W9-BGB-182

For my wife Susan, my daughters Sara Anne and
Caroline Elizabeth, and all the tiny stars waiting to shine.
"Dream, believe, persist and you will shine!"

Library of Congress Catalog Card Number: 89-62704 ISBN: 1-56288-134-5
Printed in the United States of America 0 9 8 7 6 5 4 3

Checkerboard Press, Inc.
30 Vesey Street, New York, New York 10007

THE TINY STAR

BY ARTHUR GINOLFI
ILLUSTRATED BY PAT SCHORIES

CHECKERBOARD PRESS
NEW YORK

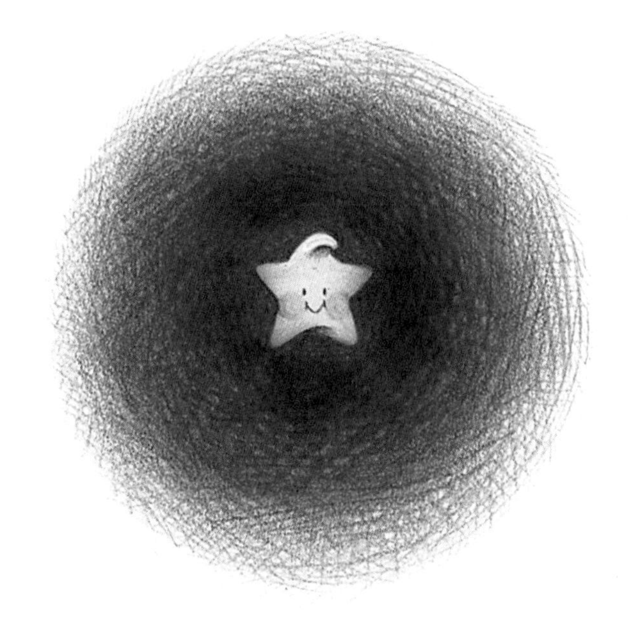

A very long time ago there was a tiny star named Starlet.

She was so small she could hardly be seen.
All the other stars were much bigger and brighter than Starlet.

At night when people looked up at the sky, they saw all the big, bright stars.

But no one ever saw Starlet.

One night Starlet asked the other stars if there was some way she could twinkle and sparkle like them.

But the stars just laughed and said, “Oh, no, Starlet. You are far too small.”

Starlet felt very sad, and she began to cry. “No one ever sees me,” she said. “I wish I were bigger.”

Later that night the wise old moon saw Starlet.

“Why are you so sad?” he asked.

"Because," said Starlet, "I try to twinkle and sparkle, but I am the smallest star in the sky, and no one ever sees me."

"Don't be sad," said the old moon gently. "How big or small you are is not important. Someday, somewhere, someone will notice you."

"But when?" asked Starlet.

The moon smiled and said, "Someday, somewhere." And he went on his way.

Many years passed. Night after night Starlet shone, but no one ever saw her.

Then one night something very strange happened.

Starlet began to fall from the sky!

Down, down, down she fell.

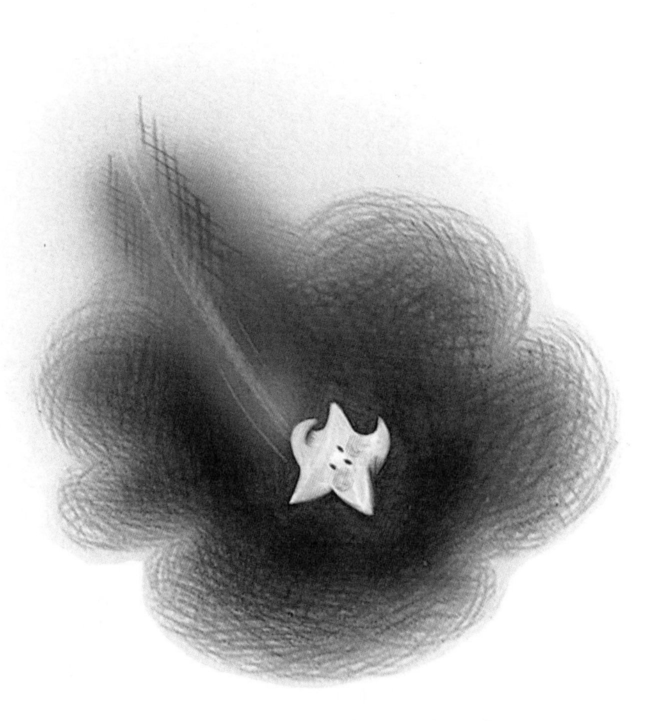

Starlet landed gently on the roof of a little stable.

Everything was dark and quiet.
The only sounds she heard were those of the animals.

Starlet felt very tired. But just as she began to fall asleep she heard a baby crying.

Starlet looked inside the stable and saw a tiny baby lying in a manger.

"Oh!" she cried. "This stable is so cold and dark. Perhaps I can shine enough to brighten it up."

So Starlet moved closer to the baby.

When the baby saw Starlet and felt the warmth of her gentle rays, he began to smile.

The more the baby smiled, the brighter Starlet shone!

The whole stable glowed.

It was a miracle.

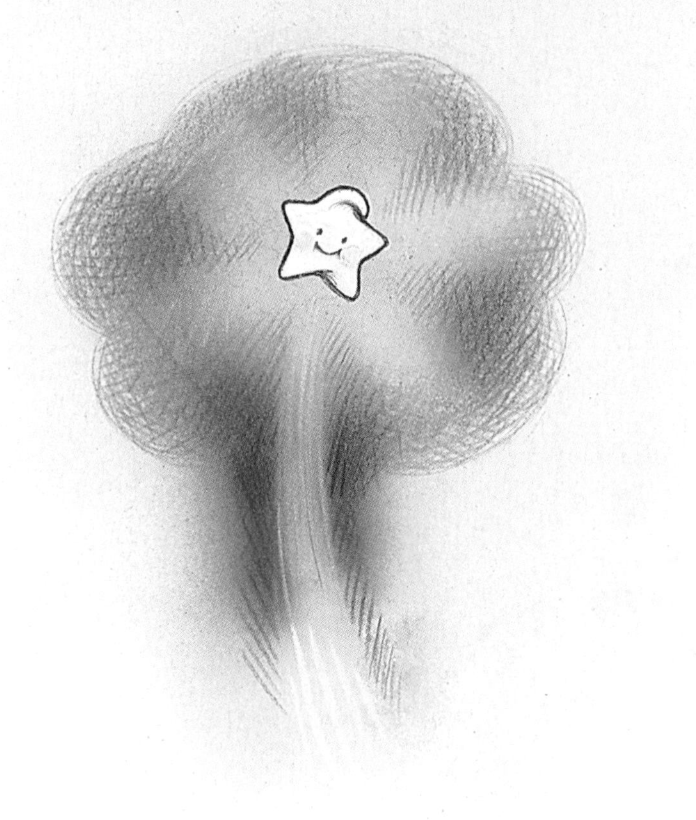

As Starlet grew brighter she began to rise.
Up, up, up into the sky, higher and higher, brighter and brighter.

Everyone saw the magnificent star.

Starlet was now the brightest star in the sky. All the other stars looked happily at her.

This was the moment she had always wished for!

And on that special night, shining over the little stable in Bethlehem, Starlet was the most beautiful star the world has ever seen.